The
MONSTER
Sale

For pupils and teachers in the Guernsey schools that have made me so welcome on many occasions.

JANETTA OTTER-BARRY BOOKS

First published in Great Britain in 2013 by
Frances Lincoln Children's Books, 74-77 White Lion Street, London N1 9PF
www.franceslincoln.com

A catalogue record for this book is available from the British Library.

ISBN 978-1-84780-366-5

Set in Charlotte Book

Printed by CPI Group (UK) Ltd, Croydon, CR0 4YY

1 3 5 7 9 8 6 4 2

The MONSTER Sale

Poems by
BRIAN MOSES

F
FRANCES LINCOLN
CHILDREN'S BOOKS

Contents

The Monster Sale

(Sign in a department store window: 'Monster Sale')

Monsters that wait behind your door,
    monsters that slither across the floor.

Monsters that moan and groan and wail,
    buy your monsters at the Monster Sale.

Monsters that bite and leave a mark,
    monsters that shine and glow in the dark.

Monsters that look like you and me,
    buy one monster get one free.

A box of monsters to put under beds,
    a sack of monsters with two or three heads.

Monsters with chipped and blackened teeth,
    monsters with baby monsters beneath.

Out-of-date monsters from the bargain bin,
    monsters that fit inside a tin.

Monsters that tap on your window at night,
  monsters that whisper, 'You're in for a fright.'

Monsters that hide in your teacher's drawer,
  such silly offers you can't ignore.

But our monsters need feeding to help them grow,
  so step this way to our basement below.

Such knock-down prices you just won't believe.
  Pity you'll never be able to leave. . .

Alive!

2 FOR 1

A Good Scary Poem Needs...

A haunted house,

a pattering mouse.

A spooky feeling,

a spider-webbed ceiling.

A squeaking door,

a creaking floor.

A swooping bat,

the eyes of a cat.

A dreadful dream,

a distant scream.

A ghost that goes **BOO**

and You!

Spooked

When your house feels strange
and you can't say why,
when you wake at night
to the echo of a cry.

When the floorboards creak
to the faintest footfall
and the temperature drops
for no reason at all.

When the rocking chair rocks
but no one's there,
when someone has triggered
your squeaky stair.

When the curtains move
and there isn't a breeze,
when the house is empty
but you hear a sneeze.

You've been spooked
by a **spook.**

Now you're host
to a **ghost!!!**

Night School

If you should visit
your school at night,
it wouldn't seem
such a friendly sight.

Open the door
and step inside.
There are so many places
where something could hide.

Then as you tiptoe
from room to room,
eyes will be peering
out from the gloom.

The hall looks empty
but look once more,
there seems to be something
behind the door.

The toilets may flush
when no one's there,
a globe spins round
in the empty air.

Footsteps may sound
as they climb the stairs.
In the silent classroom,
the scraping of chairs.

Then as you exit
you'll get a fright
when voices close by
whisper…
  Good night,
   sleep tight,
    and don't let
     the bed bugs bite….

Awake

I know I'm the only one awake in this house.
I might be the only one awake down our street.
I could be the only one awake in this town.

No! That's not right –
there'd be
policemen policing,
nurses nursing,
night watchmen watching the night.

There'd be others too, asleep,
but dreaming.
A teacher dreaming hopefully,
A bank manager dreaming fitfully,
A shop-keeper dreaming nervously,
An acrobat dreaming spinningly.

Big Bad Enid Blyton & Me

But I can't sleep and I probably won't
so I'm tuning into the stillness,
I'm floating along on a cushion of dark.
And I know...

I know I'm the only one awake in my house,
I know why too!
In five hours and 23 minutes
I can open my birthday presents.

Big Ted, Enid Blyton & Me

Big Ted, Enid Blyton and me,
we were climbing the Faraway Tree,
exploring enchanted forests
and running back home for our tea.

We'd play with the Famous Five
and be their invisible chums.
Big Ted, Enid Blyton and me
had adventures that frightened our mums.

We'd be out there chasing smugglers,
catching robbers up to no good.
Spies always got what was coming,
plans always worked out as they should.

Her books were great adventure,
happy days and laughter,
stories that we knew would end
happily ever after.

Naming the Puppy

What to call the puppy was a problem
on which we couldn't agree.
I thought Cuddles or even Puddles
but everyone outvoted me.

We thought we might call her Meg,
Cassie, Molly or Shelley.
My brother's suggestion was silly,
no way we're calling her Smelly!

Dad said let's call her 'Costalot'
because she sure cost lots of money.
But she looked so sugary sweet
that everyone said, "She's Honey!"

Me and My Dog

I'm taking my dog for a walk.
I'm teaching my dog how to talk.
I'm taking my dog for a stroll.
I'm showing my dog how to rock 'n' roll.
I'm taking my dog for a hike.
I'm teaching my dog how to ride a bike.
I'm showing my dog how to roller-skate.
I'm taking my dog on a dinner date.
Too late, she's already spoken for,
she's given her heart to the dog next door!

A Puppy's Favourite Chews

Tea towels hanging temptingly
from a hook on the cupboard door.

Feet-flavoured sweaty trainers
abandoned on the floor.

A lucky dip of forgotten socks
from the opened washing machine,

Dad's still-rolled-up newspaper
and Mum's gossip magazine.

Seat cushions that fall on the floor
and then put up a fight,

crunchy bugs and slimy slugs
from the garden late at night.

Shoe laces left dangling down
and waxy mobile phones,

and all those teeth-cracking leathery things
that look a lot like

BONES!

Worst Crimes Our Dog is Guilty Of...

Leaving a trail of very muddy footprints across the cream carpet and onto the settee.

Licking plates so clean in the open dishwasher that someone thinks the cycle has finished, takes out the plates and stacks them away.

Rolling in something incredibly stinky and then trying to share it with you by rubbing against your legs.

Bringing slugs in from the garden so they can paint silver trails on the living room carpet.

Chewing up a £20 note that falls on the floor.

Chasing anything that moves but particularly cats, squirrels, pheasants, rabbits, spiders and plastic bags.

Being far too cute for her own good.

There's Not a Lot a Labrador Won't Eat!

I've eaten May bugs and June bugs,
woodlice and ants.
I've chewed on Mum's knickers
and ripped up Dad's pants.

But munching on slugs
left my mouth full of slime,
and cabbage-white butterflies,
don't waste your time.

For the sake of research
I've tried quite a few
but the taste is
undeniably – ugh!

Anything that falls
to the floor is mine.
Don't try to retrieve it,
you won't have the time.

You'll just see a blur
as I make my dash.
I'm lightning dog,
there in a flash.

I eat what I want,
that's the labrador way.
but please be quite fussy
with your food today.

If there's food you don't like
just reach down when you're able
and guess who'll be waiting there
under the table!

When I Bark...

If you listened to me
then you'd know
that when I bark
it's...

a how dare you leave me out here bark,
a let me in I beg you bark.

A last time my tail wags for you bark,
an after everything I've done too bark.

A who do you think you are bark,
leaving me here in the dark bark.

A way overdue for a walk bark,
a let's go and run in the park bark.

A time you got off the settee bark
and paid more attention to me bark.

A where it's gone is a mystery bark,
a bet it's rolled under the furniture bark.

A come on let's go bark,
a find stick and throw bark.

a roll on the mat bark,
a warning to cats bark.

a joyful and playful
zip a dee doo bark.

a time you learnt dog language bark.

then you humans might know
exactly what I mean!

Our Dog's Response to a Leaflet about a Lost Cat

"All cats would go missing
if I had it my way
and I certainly wouldn't be using
my special powers in the nose department
to help bring them home.

They can stay lost, as far as I'm concerned.
No cats in our neighbourhood
would really suit me.
I wouldn't need to get so excited
when some cat comes on the scene
and struts about like it's descended
from an ancient Egyptian god.

If I Had Ears the Size of

Satellite Dishes a

Think again, cats, 'dog'
is 'god' spelt backwards.
These three letters are in our name
so don't try to lord it over us.

Get lost, stay missing,
keep out of my sight.
That's got to be every dog's delight.
Cats, who needs them?
Not me, not ever.
Dogs are the clever ones
and although we may roam
we always know how
to find our way
back home."

If I Had Ears the Size of Satellite Dishes...

If I had ears the size of satellite dishes...

I could hear the buzz and whine of saws
as they toppled rainforest trees.

I could hear the soft beating
of a butterfly's wings.

I could hear a ladybird's footsteps on a leaf
and the arguments of ants under the ground.

I could hear mice scampering through
    the Queen's cellars
and a dog barking in New York.

I could hear aliens bleeping their messages
    through space
and the breathing of an octopus beneath the sea.

But even with ears the size of satellite dishes,
I still wouldn't hear my mum
telling me...

TO TIDY MY ROOM!

The Frog Olympics

The news spread quickly, the word went round
from lake and ditch, across boggy ground,

To garden ponds and further still
as an audience gathered on the side of a hill

for the Frog Olympics.

And frogs of every colour and size
watched the events through big bulgy eyes.

There were frogs that had swum from across the sea,
there were tree frogs peeping from every tree,

at the Frog Olympics.

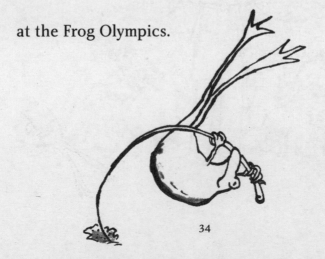

There were medals for tongues that could catch
    most flies
and the frog that hopped away with first prize

was an elderly frog whose tongue when uncurled
could stretch half-way around the world,

at the Frog Olympics.

There were medals for winning Three-Legged Frog
and for jumping in and out of a bog.

There was leapfrogging streams from bank to bank,
and skilful pole-vaulting over a plank,

at the Frog Olympics.

Then to celebrate the end of the games,
a torch was lit and they followed the flames

to a stream where the final event took place,
a fast and furious tadpole race,

at the Frog Olympics.

And oh those leaps that were so fantastic
from frogs that must have had legs of elastic.

While everyone agreed that one day soon
they might see a frog jumping over the moon.

(Well, a cow did it once, or so they say,
and so frogs keep practising, every day....)

Some Chickens Wear Jumpers

Some chickens wear jumpers,
some chickens wear tights.
Some chickens have make-overs,
some chickens have highlights.

Some chickens use
a range of perfumes.
Some chickens listen
to groovy i-tunes.

Some chickens like
to wear tight jeans.
Some chickens read
the fashion magazines.

Some chickens have
a bad-feather day.
Some chickens
always look OK.

Some chickens like
words on their vests.
(EGG POWER!)
Some chickens stay
completely undressed.

And some chickens do
what they've always done.
Just bathe in the dust
and then snooze in the sun.

(There is actually someone in Norfolk
who knits jumpers for ex battery hens
that have lost lots of feathers.)

A Bear in his Underwear

You shouldn't point and you mustn't stare
if you see a bear in his underwear.

It's really rude to take a peep
at a bear just woken from winter sleep.

A bear who's out to test the air
while wondering what clothes to wear.

For him it will be a big surprise,
he'll be trying to rub the sleep from his eyes.

He'll be thinking of honey and hoping to find
something sweet that the bees left behind.

So don't be surprised if when you wave
he disappears into his cave.

He'll really be in no mood to talk
till he's properly dressed and off for a walk.

So if you see a bear with holes in his vest
and pants a long way past their best,

Pass him by, just leave him there,
if you see a bear who's almost bare!

Dragonfly

A dragonfly will be content
    to simply float or hover.
A dragonfly is not a guy
    to give you any bother.
He won't sting you like a wasp will
    or annoy you like a fly.
A whirr of wings, a blur of blue
    and dragonfly – goodbye.

The Bug Hotel

It's a good place to find,
it's a place to unwind
at the end of each creep-crawly day.

It's a space to relax,
to order some snacks
and to plan for a very long stay.

And if you are a slug
you'll be slimy and snug,
you can sleep all winter through.

Even hide 'n' seek spiders,
those web joyriders
will not be looking for you.

At the bug hotel,
the slug hotel,
the creatures you don't want to hug hotel.

But beneath a big log
watch out for the frog
whose tongue is so long and so sticky.

He doesn't much care
who he eats so beware,
as avoiding him could be tricky.

And if you should stay,
no lights guide your way,
save the shine from a slippery moon.

But you'll be all right
and for your delight,
the beetles will strum you a tune.

At the bug hotel,
the slug hotel,
the creatures you don't want to hug hotel.

And the spiders all know
that wherever they go
they'll never be short of a meal.

While smaller bugs may
find to their dismay,
they're an 'all you can eat' special deal.

At the bug hotel,
the slug hotel,
the creatures you don't want to hug hotel.

And if you check in,
you may never check out,
there are bigger and nastier
creatures about,
than you. . . .

My Yakkety Yak

You should meet
my yakkety yak,
she's always talking
and answering back.

She's always yelling,
whining and moaning
and if she knew how
she'd be telephoning,

complaining about
how often it rains,
how cold it can be
on Mongolian plains.

She's the sort of creature
that drives me wild.
But my polar bear
is meek and mild.

(And my talking bird
hardly says a word!)

The Cow at the Back of the Queue

I'm the cow
at the back of the queue
as everyone
can see,
and even though
I moo and I moo
no one takes notice
of me.

I'm never allowed
to be leader,
to decide what we're
going to do.
I'm never allowed
first place,
I haven't a loud enough
moo.

My moo is rather pitiful
compared to all the rest.
I know I won't be a winner,
I'll never be the best.

Now her, up front,
has authority.
She always says
what to do.
Her voice is the one
we listen to,
she has that sort of
moo.

Her moo is a signal
to everyone,
"Stop chewing and
do as I say."
And I take my place
in the line,
and I think that
maybe one day

I'll turn my moo into
a moo cow hullabaloo,
so better start practising now,
it's one, two, three and then

MOO!

Fish Ladder

How could fish ever learn
to use a ladder?
They'd get madder and madder
trying not to slip on the rungs.
Fish just could not grip
with no fingers or thumbs.
And why would they need one anyway?

They don't do DIY,
they don't check gutters,
there can't be any windows to clean
underwater.

It's a mystery to me why fish need ladders
but apparently they do!

(You can see one at Pitlochry in the Scottish Highlands –
it helps them travel upstream.)

The Vietnamese Pot-Bellied pig

The Vietnamese pot-bellied pig
will never come first in a race.
He'll never win beauty contests
or be prized for his smiling face.
And as for his table manners,
they're an absolute disgrace.
But the Vietnamese pot-bellied pig
is so ugly, he's really ace!

What an Aardvark Likes to Do Best

If an aardvark asks
for a date in the dark,
don't dress up smart
for a stroll in the park.
Don't expect to be taken
to the local disco
or to visit a nightclub
in Acapulco....

For what an aardvark
likes to do best
is to hoover up ants
from a big ants' nest.

An aardvark's eyesight
is non-existent,
but this guy, well,
he's really persistent.
He'll keep on keeping
his nose to the ground
till it leads him on
to a termite mound.

For what an aardvark
likes to do best
is to stick his nose
in a termites' nest.

So if an aardvark asks you
out on a datc,
just be prepared
for a very long wait.
Sit down, get comfy
on the ground,
while he checks out
his termite mound
or hoovers ants
from a big ants' nest.
It's what an aardvark
likes to do best.

A Crocodile Called Burt

(For Karen)

He's a funky crocodile,
a chunky crocodile,
a crocodile called Burt.

He's a fearsome beast,
three metres at least,
he looks sleepy but he is alert.

Just don't be misled
that he's tired in bed,
by the sound of his rumbling snores.

If you get too near
you may well disappear
between his chewmungous jaws.

He's a moving rock,
he's a common croc,
no pedigree and no frills.

But next door you'll see
reptile royalty,
two crocs called Kate and Wills!

(There really are two crocodiles named after the
Duke and Duchess of Cambridge, and they both live
with Burt at Crocosaurus Cove, a crocodile sanctuary
in Darwin, Australia.)

A Bit of a Hiccup

There's been a bit of a hiccup,
Dad said. And I thought
of when I got hiccups,
lots of them, never
just one.

Seven years, is what it took.
Seven years in the Guinness Book
for the longest recorded bout
of hiccuping in the world.

It frightens me, every time
I start to hiccup, I always think
I'm setting out on
a record-beating attempt.

Hic-hic-hicupping
all day long...

Only another 6 years, 364 days,
23 hours and forty-seven minutes
of hic-hic-hicupping,
oh, wait a minute…

they've gone!

Pleasant Street

(For everyone at VCP, the school on Pleasant Street in Jersey)

How pleasant to live on Pleasant Street
where nobody gets annoyed,
where news is always good
and the residents overjoyed
to live in such a street
where raised voices are seldom heard,
where arguments never happen
and no one speaks a cross word.

There are no takers in Pleasant Street
for everyone learns how to give.
No one ever moves from Pleasant Street
for where else could they live?
Once you've seen the warmth of its welcome,
once you've felt the sun on your shoulder,
once you've found out how young you stay
and how nobody grows any older.

I'd love to live on Pleasant Street
where no one complains about money,
where happiness spreads like sunshine
and gleams like golden honey.
For everyone here knows that laughter
is really good for your health.
To offer the gift of laughter shows
a special kind of wealth.

How pleasant to see smiles everywhere
and nobody wearing a frown.

I'd love to discover Pleasant Street
in every city and town.

The Language of Rollercoasters

You don't need to go to school to learn
the language of rollercoasters.

You won't need a dictionary
to help you with awkward words,
and there are no tests
to show teachers how well you've done.

The language of rollercoasters
is not a difficult one.
You won't have to think about
what you'll say....

For as you ride to the top of the hill
and the train spills over
in a mighty thrill,
your mouth will open
and the words you need
will twirl from beneath
your tongue

Oooooooooooooo
　aaaaahhhhhhhh
　　Urghhhhhhhhhh
　　　Oh noooooooooo
Help meeeeeeee
　Mummeeeeeeeee
　　Wheeeeeeeeeeee!
　　　Yippeeeeeeeeeee

and the final, most important ones,

"Let's go on it again!"

When the Queen Came to Tea

When the Queen came to tea,
Dad had just finished dusting
and was brushing the red carpet.

Mum was a mess, she hadn't had time
to change her dress.

When the Queen came to tea,
we picked up her crown
and flicked it onto a hook.

We passed round Mum's best plates
and she ate two slices of chocolate cake.

When the Queen came to tea,
Grandma kept saying, "She's just the same
as she is on the telly."
Grandad gave her a bottle
of his peapod wine.

When the Queen came to tea
the dog ran to hide, then brought her the bone
that he'd hidden in the garden.

All the neighbours found excuses
to call round.

When the Queen came to tea
my sister gave her a party bag,

she wrote her name in my book,

she needed to use our bathroom.

When the Queen came to tea...

she was lovely!

Superman's Sister

Our mum must be Superman's sister,
we're amazed at what she does.

Fighting monstrous piles of washing,
battling the bulky duvets,
taming the horror that's our Hoover,
rescuing us from those terrifying spiders,
wrestling the dog who never wants to be brushed,
finding Big Bunny who's always *on the run*,

and,
dashing at streak-of-lightning speed
to save us all from being late for school!

First and Last

I'm the last one at school in the morning
and first out the door at night,
I'm the first one in the dinner queue
but the last to get my maths right.

I'm the last to help tidy up
and the first to switch on the TV,
I'm the last to get out of bed
and the first to finish my tea.

I'm the last to jump in the water
when we stand at the edge of the pool,
I'm first to the ice-cream van
when it waits outside my school.

I'm the last to finish my homework
and the first to the shop for sweets,
I'm the last to volunteer
but the first in line for treats!

I'm the last to do what I'm told
and it makes my teacher shout,
but if friends of mine are in trouble
I'll be first to help them out.

The Gunge Tank (Summer Fete)

The very best gunge in the whole world
is made from

spaghetti,
curry powder,
mouldy cake crumbs,
lumpy custard,
dead earwigs,
picked-off scabs
and
pond slime. . .

all mixed together in a canteen container
with the dregs of last Tuesday's brown stew.
And what do you do
with the very best gunge in the world
once you've made it?

You pour it all over
your very best teacher,
what else?

All in a good cause,
of course!

The Dungeons

We saw turrets and towers,
a bridge and a moat,
blackened brick ovens
and the Mayor's coat.

But, I wanted to see the dungeons....

We saw pottery in pieces,
brooches and pins,
Roman coins
and animal skins.

But, I wanted to see the dungeons....

We saw shiny armour
and paintings of kings,
Egyptian writing
and ancient brass rings.

But, I wanted to see the dungeons....

Then at last we went down
to a tiny room
where they turned out the lights
and left us in the gloom.

They rattled some chains
and we heard ghostly groans,
the creaking of doors,
mumblings and moans.

Now I wish I hadn't seen the dungeons,
I wish we had just gone home!

Body Double

(Some famous film stars use "body doubles"– actors who look like them – to be in any scenes that they don't want to take part in.)

Do I have to?
It's too much trouble.
I wish I had
a body double.

Someone who
could help me out
when all around me
begin to shout.

Someone who
could take the blame
when my teacher burns
as hot as a flame.

If someone threatened
to give me a thrashing,
my body double
could take the bashing.

I could stay in bed
while he went to school,
he could get cold
in the swimming pool.

He could always do
the things that I hate
and eat up the food
that I leave on my plate.

A body double
would really be ace.
What a look there'd be
on my teacher's face,

when normally good
and quiet me
goes haywire, flips out
totally.

A body double
would really be fun,
but the problem is,
where do I find one?

Walking Energy

I lose my walking energy
when someone suggests
a hike in the park,
a walk after lunch,
a stroll before dark.

I feel it flowing
out of me,
all my walking energy.

So I won't mind
if you want to take
a walk by the sea
without me,
a stroll on the grass,
I'll let it pass,
a hike down the street,
I'll save my feet,
but you,
you can do as you like.

Till someone suggests
we bypass the bus
and walk to the shops
where I can buy
a brand new toy for me...

It's then I find,
remarkably,
that all my walking energy
is suddenly
back with me!

Dunking

I have to admit it,
I do like dunking biscuits.

But it's a gamble, a risk
each time I dunk,
a thin line
between failure and success.

A thin line between
dunking delight and
dunking disaster.

Dunked properly
I can savour the flavour
of the biscuit.

Dunked carelessly
it will thicken my tea.

But I do like dunking biscuits
(especially the chocolate ones).

Tyres

Do tyres get tired of the road,
travelling mile after mile,
carrying heavy loads?

I wondered about this today
when I found old tyres
that had long ago given up
the touch of rubber on road.

Tyres all together
in some old tyres' home,
talking of roads,
the journeys they've known.

Huge tyres telling of tractor days,
one time stuck in mud,
another tipped into a stream.

Tyres dreaming,
going somewhere again,
instead of just old and
retired from the road.

Tank Training

Down in Dorset
on the army range,
I saw a sign that said,
TANK TRAINING DAYS.

And I wondered,
how do you train a tank?

How do you teach it
to behave...?

Tell it not to point its barrel at people,
tell it not to make loud noises,
tell it not to puff out smoke
or spit fire.

And how do you make it
do what you want?

Offer it treats?

Here tanky tanky,
nice tanky tanky!

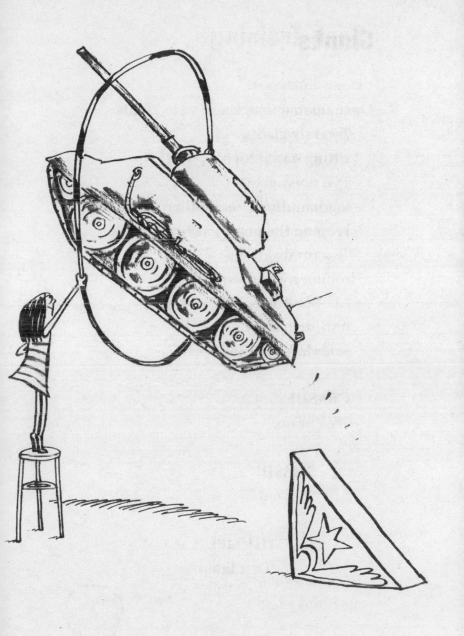

Giants

Once upon a time there were giants. . . .
    Two lazy giants
    sitting on hilltops.
    Two noisy giants
    loudmouthing each other all night,
    keeping the nearby villages awake.
    Two rowdy giants
    rolling rocks down valleys
    like bowling balls,
    hurling insults
    scrawled on boulders:

CRASH!
"Pea brain."

    SMASH!
    "Big nut."

        THUMP!
        "Daft lump."

And if you were unlucky enough
to wander into the flight path
of boulders from angry giants
you'd be bowled over,
squashed flat,
lost from sight.

But of course there wouldn't have been
quite so many broken bones
if only these two giants
had had mobile phones!

If I Were a Shape

If I were a shape,

I'd be a rectangle.
I'd be a snooker table with a champion
potting the black,
I'd be a football pitch where Spurs
would always be winning,
I'd be a chocolate bar you could never finish,
If I were a rectangle.

If I were a circle,
I'd be a hoop rolling down a mountainside,
I'd be a wheel on a fast Ferrari,
I'd be a porthole in Captain Nemo's submarine,
If I were a circle.

If I were a cone,
I'd be a black hat on a wicked witch's head,
I'd be a warning to motorists, one of thousands,
I'd be a tooth in a T Rex's jaw,
If I were a cone.

But if I were a star...
I'd be Lady Gaga!

I Wouldn't Want To Be...

I wouldn't want to be a cow
when it's just about to rain.
or a pesky younger brother
and always be labelled a pain.

I wouldn't want to be a dog biscuit
when a labrador's looking for lunch
or a boxer in the ring
receiving a knockout punch.

I wouldn't want to be a fly
about to become a spider's meal,
or a shadowy shape of a ghost
and know I could never be real.

I wouldn't want to be a dandelion
when the mower comes along,
or a red-faced politician
who is always told he's wrong...

I wouldn't want to be chewing gum
stuck to someone's shoe,
and I wouldn't want to be a lavatory brush
that gets poked head first down the loo...

Well, would you?

Travelling to the Beat of a Drum

Hear the sound of your feet
as you walk down the street
when you travel to the beat of a drum.

Hear a guitar's strum
hear machinery thrum
when you travel to the beat of a drum.

Hear fingers start snapping
hear toes tip-tapping,
hear a city's heartbeat
through the summer heat
when you travel to the beat of a drum.

Hear the sound of a flute,
hear the rooty-toot-toot,
hear the pad of a cat,
hear the people chitchat,
hear the slap of a shoe,
hear the noise that is you
when you travel to the beat of a drum.

Hear fire burning,
hear the whole world turning
when you travel to the beat of a drum,
when you travel to the beat of a drum.

So beat that rhythm,
make it sound for me,
if you're in the city
or by the sea,
if you're out on the town,
when you're up and not down

Just travel to the beat of a drum,
everybody,
let's travel to the beat of a drum.

Any Regrets?

Do crocodiles cry tears
because they're sorry
for people they've eaten?

Do footballers show sympathy
for the sides that
they've just beaten?

Does a blackbird feel pity
for worms that
wriggle in his belly?

Does a skunk feel dismayed
when someone says
he's smelly?

Do dragons feel regret
for the knights that
they've just roasted?

Does the sun feel sorry
for the sunbathers
it toasted?

Do cats feel upset
when their claws

imprison birds?

And do poets feel unhappy
when they're suddenly
lost for ....

BRIAN MOSES has been labelled 'one of Britain's
favourite children's poets' by the National Poetry
Archive. He has worked as a professional poet since
1988 and continues to perform his poetry and
percussion show in schools, libraries, theatres and
festivals around the UK and abroad. He was asked by
CBBC to write a poem for the Queen's 80th Birthday,
invited by Prince Charles to speak at the Prince's
Summer conference at Cambridge University and is a
'Reading Champion' for the National Literacy Trust.
He has written or edited over 200 books and
The Monster Sale is his first poetry collection
for Frances Lincoln.

www.brianmoses.co.uk

978-1-84780-269-9 • PB • £5.99

Funny, fantastic, outrageous, wise. . .
a powerful mix of comic and serious verse
from one of the UK's most popular poets.

"wild and witty" – *Telegraph*

978-1-84780-367-2 • PB • £6.99

A new collection of fizzy, sparkling poems
for younger children by award-winning author,
Wes Magee.

Here are poems with rhythm and rhyme
about friends and families, pets and creatures,
school, space travel, holidays, games, bedtime,
the seasons and Christmas.

978-1-84780-321-4 • PB • £5.99

This brilliant collection is full of wit,
wordplay and wisdom from Roger McGough...

"A word juggler who never misses a catch"
Charles Causley